Scoop Doogan and Skip Malone
and the
Case of the
Smoke Bomber

Don Keown

High Noon Books
Novato, California

Cover Design and Illustrations: Herb Heidinger

Glossary: different, government, politics, rotten, tough, typewriter, suitcase

International Standard Book Number: 0-87879-438-7

5 4 3 2 1 0 9 8 7 6
2 1 0 9 8 7 6 5 4 3

Contents

CHAPTER 1

Scoop Doogan Gets a Letter

Skip Malone rushed out of his last class at Big City High. He made sure he had gum for Scoop Doogan, star reporter at the Big City Times. He didn't want to be late for his job at the Big City Times newspaper.

As soon as he got there he passed out the mail in the news room. Scoop Doogan got a big pile of letters. He didn't look happy.

"What's wrong? Aren't you glad you got all that mail?" Skip asked.

"Most of these letters look like junk mail," he said. Then he looked at one letter. "But this one looks different," he said.

He opened the letter. Then he read it.

"Yes. This one is different," he said.

"Who is the letter from? And what does it say?" Skip asked.

Sometimes Skip helped Scoop when he covered the big news stories for the Big City Times. They liked working with each other.

"I'll read it to you," Scoop said.

Then he read the letter out loud. "Mr. Doogan, as you know Phillip Stone is planning to hold a meeting in Big City tomorrow. He better call off that meeting. If he tries to hold it we will see that it doesn't turn out well."

"Who signed that letter?" Skip asked.

"It's signed by The People Against Bad Government," Scoop said.

"Who is this Phillip Stone?" Skip asked.

"Phil Stone has been the head of the State Patrol. But now he is running for governor of the state," Scoop said.

"Would he make a good state governor?" Skip asked his older friend.

"Yes. I think that he would," Scoop said.

"Then why would The People Against Bad Government be against Mr. Stone? Why would they want to try to ruin his meeting in Big City?" Skip asked.

Scoop Doogan put a new stick of chewing gum into his mouth. He chewed hard. Skip knew that meant his friend was thinking hard. He waited for Scoop to speak out.

Then Scoop said, "I think that the people who sent the letter are not really against bad government at all. I think that they are against good government."

"Then who do you think these people are?" Skip asked.

"When Phil Stone was head of the State Patrol he was very tough on the crooks. I think that now the crooks are out to get even with him," Scoop answered.

"Maybe it is the man who is running for

governor against Phil Stone," Skip said.

"I don't think so. The other man is Jim Allen. He is a business man. And he is a good and fair man, too," Scoop said.

"What if Phil Stone's meeting in Big City doesn't go well? Will it ruin his chances to be governor?" Skip asked.

"Yes. It will. A lot of the voters in our state live in Big City. Phil Stone needs those votes to win," Scoop said.

"What kind of meeting is it going to be?" Skip asked next.

"It's called a rally. Phil Stone hopes that lots of people will come. And that they will then vote for him for our governor," Scoop said.

"What could the crooks do at the rally?" Skip asked.

Scoop chewed his gum some more. Then he said, "I don't know. But there are a lot of bad things that they could do."

Just then Mr. Mills, the editor of the Big City Times, yelled to Scoop from the other side of the big news room. "Scoop, come over here to my desk for a minute.

Scoop walked across the news room.

"Look at this," Mr. Mills said. Then the editor handed Scoop a piece of paper. It was a news story from Rock Falls, a city in another part of the state.

"Where did this come from?" Scoop asked.

"It just came in over the news wire," Mr. Mills said.

Scoop Doogan read the story. It told how Phil Stone's rally in Rock Falls the night before had been ruined.

"Some one shot off smoke bombs. I bet that is what they are going to do in Big City, too," Scoop Doogan told the editor of the Big City Times.

CHAPTER 2

Skip Gets Interested In Politics

"What makes you think they are going to shoot off smoke bombs here in Big City, too?" Mr. Mills asked his star reporter.

Then Scoop Doogan told him about the letter that he had just opened. "It was signed by The People Against Bad Government. But I think it came from the crooks," Scoop said.

"This could be very bad for Phil Stone. And it could make Big City look bad to people in other cities," Mr. Mills said.

"This story says that no one was hurt in Rock Falls. But there will be a lot more people at the rally here in Big City," Scoop said.

"Yes. So people might get hurt if they are scared by the smoke bombs," Mr. Mills said.

Then he told Scoop, "We must do everything we can to keep the crooks from ruining the meeting. People have a right to listen to the men and women who are asking for their votes."

"I feel that way, too," Scoop said.

"You can work as much as you need to on this story. Find out who is behind the smoke bombs. We must not let them do in Big City what they did in Rock Falls," Mr. Mills said.

Scoop went back to his desk. He told Skip what Mr. Mills had said. "And he said that you can help me on the story," Scoop said.

"Good. I'm ready. What should we do first?" Skip asked.

Scoop laughed. "You don't waste any time. Well, you're right. We should get busy on the story right away. And first we will go and have a talk with Jeff Bishop."

"Who is Jeff Bishop?" Skip asked.

"He is a lawyer. He is in charge of the rally here in Big City. He is working hard for votes for Phil Stone," Scoop said.

"Then we should go talk to Jeff Bishop right away," Skip said.

Scoop and Skip walked out to Scoop's red sports car. On their way they passed a big poster. Someone had put it on a telephone pole.

The poster said: "There is a rally tomorrow at 8 o'clock in Big City Hall."

The poster said: "There is a rally tomorrow at 8 o'clock in Big City Hall. Come and hear Phillip Stone."

Skip said to Scoop, "I've seen lots of posters like that one. And I have seen lots of stories about politics in the Big City Times. But I have never really been interested in politics before. I think that I will be after this is over."

"Yes. Everyone should be interested in politics. Even those who are not yet old enough to vote. The people who get elected make our laws. And then see that they are carried out," Scoop said.

They got into Scoop's sports car.

Scoop drove a few blocks. Skip always liked

to ride in Scoop's sports car. It was a great car. And Scoop was a good driver. Then Scoop parked the car. He pointed to a big building. "That is where Jeff Bishop does his work. He is a lawyer most of the time. But right now he is working full time for Phil Stone," Scoop said.

Scoop and Skip went inside the building.

They found Jeff Bishop at his desk.

"Hello, Scoop. It's nice to see you. Who is this with you?" Jeff Bishop asked.

"This is Skip Malone. He works for the Big City Times after school. And he helps me with some of my stories," Scoop said.

"Fine. So what can I do for you two?" Jeff Bishop asked Scoop and Skip.

Scoop told Jeff Bishop about the letter he got at the Big City Times. "The writers said that they are going to ruin your meeting here in Big City," Scoop said.

"They tried to ruin Phil Stone's rally in Rock Falls last night," Skip said.

"Yes. I heard about the smoke bombs that they shot off there," Jeff Bishop said.

"We think that they are going to try to do the same thing here," Skip said.

"They can try. But we will be ready for them here," Jeff Bishop said.

"Are you sure?" Scoop asked.

"Yes. There will be a lot of police at Big City Hall tomorrow night. And we will have some of our own people there, too. They will be watching for the crooks to show up," Jeff Bishop said.

Scoop, Skip and Jeff Bishop talked some more. But Jeff Bishop was sure that the crooks would not be able to ruin the Big City rally.

"All right. I just hope you are right," Scoop said. He and Skip got ready to leave.

"Don't worry. I am right about this. We're going to make sure that everything is OK," Jeff Bishop told him.

CHAPTER 3

A Visit To Red Grogan's Pool Hall

Scoop Doogan and Skip Malone got back into Scoop's red sports car. They talked.

"Jeff Bishop seems sure that the crooks will not be able to ruin Phil Stone's big meeting," Skip said.

"I'm afraid he is too sure," Scoop said.

"What do you mean?" Skip asked.

"There will be a lot of people in the hall tomorrow night. The police cannot watch all of them all of the time," Scoop said.

"You are right. It would be too big of a job for them," Skip said.

"Maybe we can give them some help before the rally," Scoop said.

"What do you mean? How can we do that?" Skip asked.

"We can try to find out before the meeting who is planning to ruin it. Then maybe we can scare them off," Scoop said.

"But we don't know who the crooks will send to the meeting," Skip said.

Scoop put some chewing gum into his mouth. He started chewing. "Just think. Who here in Big City would the crooks pick to do their dirty work? Who is a crook himself?"

Skip had to think for only a second. Then he answered, "Red Grogan, the man who owns the pool hall down the street. He is the worst crook in Big City."

"That is right. And I think that we are going to talk to Red Grogan," Scoop said.

Scoop started up his car. He began driving down the street.

Scoop parked his car in front of Red Grogan's Pool Hall. Inside they could see young boys playing pool and sitting around talking.

"Those boys would be better off in school. Or with jobs like the one you have at the Big City Times, Skip," Scoop Doogan said.

Scoop and Skip got out of the sports car.

They walked into the pool hall. A man came to meet them. "What are you two doing here? I do not want you in my pool hall."

"What are you two doing here?
I do not want you in my pool hall."

"We don't like being here. But we want to ask you a question," Scoop said.

"Ask it. Then get out," Red Grogan said.

"Are you going to be at Phil Stone's rally tomorrow night?" Scoop asked.

"What's it to you? I have the right to go to the rally," Red Grogan said.

"Yes. If you go for the right reason. But I don't think that you are interested in voting," Scoop said.

Skip had been looking around the pool hall at the boys who were there. They were a bad bunch. "Will you be taking any of these kids with you to the meeting?"

"What's it to you?" Red Grogan said.

Just then a man walked into the pool hall. He had parked a truck outside. On it was a sign: "Big City Fruit and Vegetable Company."

The man walked up to Red Grogan. "Where do you want me to put the stuff?" he asked.

"Put it in the room at the back of the pool hall," Red Grogan told the man.

The man left the pool hall. Then he came back. He was carrying some heavy sacks.

"Don't carry that stuff through my pool hall. Drive around to the alley. Then you can walk through the back door into the back room," Red Grogan said to the man.

Red Grogan looked at Scoop and Skip. "Are you two still here?"

"I want to say one more thing," Scoop said.

"Say it. And then leave," Red Grogan said.

"We are going to talk to the police. We are going to ask them to keep their eyes on you and the boys at the rally," Scoop said.

Red Grogan did not look happy. But he said, "You don't scare me. I have a right to go to the rally if I want to. And so do the boys. We can go there if we want!"

"Yes. But there are things you don't have the right to do there," Scoop said.

Scoop and Skip left the pool hall. They got into Scoop's red sports car. Scoop put some new chewing gum into his mouth. "Well, what do you think?" he asked Skip.

"I think Red is planning something," Skip said.

"Why do you say that?" Scoop asked.

"It was the fruit and vegetables the man took into the pool hall," Skip said.

"Yes. I thought that was funny. Red Grogan does not sell fruit in his pool hall. He only sells drinks and junk food," Scoop said.

"Something else about that stuff was even funnier. It was the way it smelled," Skip said.

"Yes. It did smell funny," Scoop said.

"I think that the fruit and vegetables were rotten," Skip said.

"But why would Red Grogan want to buy rotten fruit and vegetables?" Scoop asked.

"Well, not to eat for sure. But maybe to throw at some one," Skip answered.

"I see what you mean. Red Grogan will give that rotten stuff to his tough kids. He will send them to Phil Stone's meeting. And they will throw the fruit and vegetables at Mr. Stone when he speaks," Scoop said.

"It will ruin the meeting," Skip said.

Scoop chewed on his gum. He was thinking. Then he said, "We will put a stop to that. We will go back to the Big City Times. I'll call the police and tell them about the rotten fruit.

"Will the police care?" Skip asked.

"I don't know. But I'm sure the city health people will," Scoop said.

24

CHAPTER 4

Two Visitors To The News Room

Scoop Doogan and Skip Malone were back in the Big City Times news room. First Scoop talked to Mr. Mills, the editor. He told him what they had found out.

Then he called the police. He told them about the rotten fruit at the pool hall.

Then Scoop told Skip, "That will take care of Red Grogan. The police said they will tell the city health people about the rotten fruit and vegetables at the pool hall."

Then Scoop and Skip had other work to do. Scoop had other stories to write. Skip had lots of things to do for the reporters and editors.

Scoop had to stop his work two times when he had visitors. The first visitor was a tall man in a gray suit.

He walked over to Scoop's desk.

"Mr. Doogan? I'm Jim Allen," the man said.

"Yes, Mr. Allen. You are running against Phil Stone for the job of governor," Scoop said.

"I'm giving a talk tonight in a town near here. But I heard about the letter that you got. That some one was trying to spoil Mr. Stone's rally here tomorrow," Jim Allen said.

"Yes. I did get a letter," Scoop said.

"Well, I want to tell you something. I had nothing to do with that letter. I do not like that way of trying to get votes," Jim Allen said.

"I believe you," Scoop Doogan said.

"The people will not like it. It might lose me votes. That would not help me to become the new governor," Jim Allen said.

"That's true. I know that you are a fair person. And I will say so in the Big City Times," Scoop told Jim Allen.

"Thank you," Jim Allen said.

Then Scoop told Jim Allen about Red Grogan at the pool hall. And about the rotten fruit and vegetables there.

Scoop pointed to Skip, "I think my young helper Skip there and I have put a stop to that. We told the police about Red Grogan."

He was carrying a suitcase and a typewriter case.

"That is good. Throwing stuff would not be as bad as the smoke bombs at Rock Falls. But it would still be very bad," Jim Allen said.

Jim Allen and Scoop Doogan talked some more. Then Jim Allen left.

A minute later another man walked into the news room. He was carrying a suitcase and a typewriter case. He stopped at Scoop's desk.

"Mr. Doogan? I am Joe Rush of the American News Service. I write about politics. And I came here for Phil Stone's big meeting tomorrow night," the man said.

Scoop Doogan and Joe Rush shook hands.

"I know. The American News Service covers stories all over the country," Scoop said.

"Yes. Our editors thought we should cover the Big City rally. What happened in Rock Falls has made everyone interested in it," Joe Rush said.

"What can I do to help you?" Scoop asked.

"I thought you could tell me how to get in touch with Phil Stone's people. I need a ticket for the rally. And also tell me where the best hotel in Big City might be," Joe Rush said.

"Skip Malone, our copy boy, can help you with both of those things," Scoop Doogan said.

He called Skip over to his desk. Skip and Joe Rush shook hands. Then Scoop asked Skip to call the Big City Hotel. He was to get a good room for Joe Rush. And to call Jeff Bishop. He was to ask for a front row ticket for Joe Rush.

"Tell Jeff Bishop that Joe needs to be close to the speakers," Scoop told Skip.

Skip made the telephone calls. Then he told Joe Rush, "You have a good room at the Big City Hotel for tonight. And you have a good seat at Phil Stone's rally tomorrow night."

Joe Rush thanked Skip. Then he said, "I think I should walk over to Jeff Bishop's office. I would like to talk to him." He picked up his suitcase and the typewriter case.

"I could take those over to the hotel. They would be there waiting for you," Skip said.

"No. They are too heavy for you. And I am used to carrying them," Joe said. Then he left.

"I didn't think the American News Service would send a reporter to the rally," Skip said.

"It has become a big meeting. But for the wrong reason. For what might happen there. Not for what Phil Stone might say," Scoop said.

Scoop's telephone rang. He talked. Then he hung up the phone. "That was good news"

"What was the call about?" Skip asked.

"It was from the police. They told the city's health people about all that rotten fruit at Red Grogan's Pool Hall," Scoop said.

"What happened?" Skip asked.

"They made Red Grogan get rid of it. They told him he could not keep it in a place where people buy things to eat and drink," Scoop said.

CHAPTER 5

At The Big Political Rally

Scoop Doogan and Skip Malone drove to the Big City Hall early the next night. But a lot of people were already there.

"This is going to be a big rally," Skip said.

They met Joe Rush of the American News Service outside in the hall.

He had his suitcase and his typewriter case with him. "I have to catch a train right after this meeting. I have another story to cover in another city," he told Scoop and Skip.

Skip took the typewriter case from Joe Rush. "I will carry it inside for you," he said.

They went inside the hall.

Skip took the typewriter case from Joe Rush.

"I sure hope that nothing bad happens here tonight. It wouldn't be good with this many people," Scoop said.

"Well, you and Skip have taken care of your Big City crook, Red Grogan. I don't think that he will show up tonight," Joe Rush said.

"Yes. But you never can tell. The crooks who hate Phil Stone will not give up," Scoop said.

Scoop and Skip helped Joe Rush get to his seat. Then they went to their own seats. They were also sitting in the front row.

Scoop and Skip waited for the rally to begin.

Scoop was chewing gum. He looked around the big hall. "I don't see Red Grogan."

"Yes. I think they have been scared away. But I don't think that they are the main ones to be watched," Skip said.

"What do you mean?" Scoop asked.

"I think we should watch Joe Rush," Skip said.

"Joe Rush? Why should we watch a reporter from the American News Service?" Scoop asked.

"I don't think that Joe Rush is a real news reporter," Skip answered.

Scoop Doogan was surprised. "Why do you say that?" he asked Skip.

"There is no typewriter in that case he has with him. The case is too light. I could tell that when I carried it for him," Skip said.

"Yes. Even a small typewriter is very heavy," Scoop said.

"I think that the typewriter case is packed with smoke bombs," Skip said.

"You could be right," Scoop said.

"And that is why he brought his suitcase with him to the meeting hall. He wants to make a quick get away after the smoke bombs go off," Skip said.

"Another thing is funny. Joe Rush knew all about Red Grogan when he saw us tonight. We didn't tell him about Red. He must have talked to Red Grogan himself. They work together," Scoop said.

Then they saw Jeff Bishop.

Jeff was walking out onto the stage of Big City Hall. Another man was with him. He was Phil Stone, the man who wanted to be governor.

"The rally is about to begin," Scoop said.

The people were clapping and yelling for Phil Stone. But Skip was watching someone else.

"Joe Rush is leaving his seat. He is going to the back of the hall. And he is taking the typewriter case and suitcase with him," he said.

"Quick. We must follow him," Scoop said.

Scoop and Skip got out of their seats, too. They rushed to the back of the hall.

Behind them Phil Stone was getting ready to start his talk. But right now they were interested in Joe Rush.

CHAPTER 6

Inside The Typewriter Case

At first Scoop Doogan and Skip Malone couldn't find Joe Rush at the back of the hall. There were a lot of people all around them. Then they saw him. The man who said he was an American News Service reporter was bending down. He was opening his typewriter case.

They walked over to him.

"This is a funny place to write your story, Joe. And Phil Stone hasn't even started his talk yet," Scoop said to him.

Joe Rush was surprised to see Scoop and Skip, "Oh, hello. I wanted to check on my typewriter."

"Open up the case then. Let's all have a look at your typewriter," Scoop said.

"I have already done that. It's all right. I'm ready to go back to the meeting," Joe Rush said.

"I don't think that you are here to listen to Phil Stone talk," Scoop said. Then he grabbed the case from Joe Rush. He opened it.

There was no typewriter. Instead inside the case were what looked like big firecrackers. They were all packed together.

"Those look like smoke bombs. I've seen them before," Skip said.

The man who called himself Joe Rush started to run for the door. But Scoop was too fast for him. He grabbed him. And he held him.

*"Those look like smoke bombs.
I've seen them before," Skip said.*

The fake reporter tried hard to get away. But Scoop was too strong for him.

"Go get a policeman, Skip. This man is not going to shoot off any smoke bombs tonight," he said.

"Don't do that. The people I work for will pay you well if you will let me go," Joe Rush said.

"That proves you are not a real reporter. You would know that you cannot buy us off," Scoop said.

Skip found two policemen. He brought them back. They put handcuffs on an angry Joe.

"Smoke bombs don't hurt anyone," Joe Rush said.

"No. But smoke bombs scare people. And scared people could hurt each other badly trying to get out of that hall," Scoop said.

The two policemen took Joe Rush away.

"I can see the crooks' plans now. Red Grogan's kids were going to throw rotten fruit at the stage. Everyone would be watching that. Then Joe Rush was going to slip away to the back of the hall and shoot off the smoke bombs," Scoop said.

"Yes. If we had been watching Red Grogan's gang we would never have seen Joe Rush slip back here. Their plans were ruined when they lost their rotten fruit and vegetables," Skip said as he turned to Scoop.

"Well, I will have two stories to write. One about the smoke bombs that did not go off. Another about Phil Stone's talk. So let's go back and listen to the talk," Scoop said.

"Yes. I never thought that politics could be this interesting," Skip said.